For Cecile.
May time leave your
sense of humor unchanged.

Jean-François

ISBN: 978-1-941302-54-5
Library of Congress Control Number: 2018931218

10 9 8 7 6 5 4 3 2 1

David Sala
Jean-François Chabas

The Enchanted Chest

Many years ago, in a very distant land, a fisherman tossed a net out from his boat. When he tried to pull it back in, he found it difficult, because the net was heavy enough to tilt his whole barge.

"Ho, ho," he rejoiced. "A good catch!"

But there were no fish in his net. Just a large metal chest, which shined in the sunlight.

The fisherman tried to force open the lock with his barge pole. He pushed and pushed . . . and the pole broke, but the chest wasn't even scratched.

"As soon as I get back home, I'll find some tools to open it," he thought.

The fisherman spent hours and hours trying to open the chest. It was magnificent and made of an unknown metal that shined like the scales of a barracuda. Its lock, just as beautiful, was simple but impossible to break.

With all the noise he was making, hitting the chest and shouting at it, the fisherman drew the attention of all the other villagers. "Where did you find that chest, fisherman?" they asked him.

He didn't even take the time to respond. He continued hitting the chest and scowling. Then he heard a voice, louder and more commanding than the others.

"Well, well, what a beautiful chest! It was so nice of you, my good man, to have found such a nice present for the Emperor!"

Finally lifting his head, the fisherman saw the captain of the guard.

The Emperor reigned over much of the world. He was a terrible man and possessed one of the worst flaws: he was greedy. But despite his wealth, he still sought to amass more gold, more jewels, and more money.

He imposed taxes that left his people starving and sent his minions out across the land in search of treasure.

To the fisherman's misfortune, the captain of the guard was one of the Emperor's more zealous servants. Woe to those who would resist. So, heartbroken, the fisherman gave the chest to the captain.

"It's yours."

The Emperor sat on his throne, alone, as usual. He had never married because he believed a wife would have been far too expensive. Not to mention a child.

"What do you have there?" he asked the captain of the guard, who had requested an audience.

The captain set the chest down at the base of the throne.

"This, Your Grace."

"A chest. Where did you find it?"

The captain explained, and then, uncomfortably, he said, "Just one detail, Your Majesty. I haven't been able to open it."

"What do you mean?" exclaimed the Emperor. "How ridiculous! Break the lock with your sword!"

"I already tried, Your Highness," said the captain.

And to prove his claim, he showed his blade, which was chipped and bent.

"The chest is too solid. I only dared bring it to you because of its beauty. As for what's inside . . ."

"All my servants are useless," murmured the Emperor.

He stepped down from his throne, bent over the chest, and with all his strength, hit the lock with his scepter. The scepter broke in half.

"Aargh! My scepter! My beautiful scepter!" screamed the Emperor in anguish. "It's your fault!" he told the captain. "You will be whipped ten times!"

"But, Your Majesty—"

"But nothing! Ten lashes! On the way to your whipping, call for the jeweler to come and fix my scepter, and have the locksmith bring his tools to open this accursed chest!"

In all the Emperor's lands, the locksmith was the most skilled artisan in his field. He arrived in the throne room with his enormous toolbox.

"What can I do for Your Magnificence?" he asked.

Impatient, the Emperor pointed to the chest.

"Open this for me."

"Consider it done, Your Majesty."

But though the locksmith boasted of his skills, hours passed, and he turned white, as the Emperor reddened.

He tried a thousand keys, a thousand tools, but the chest and its lock remained unopened.

Suddenly, the Emperor exclaimed, "Idiot! Go have yourself ten lashes! And on your way out, tell the strongman to appear before me."

The strongman had to lower his head to fit through the door that led into the throne room. He was quite a large fellow, tall and big. He coughed. The sound resonated throughout the room like a wildcat's growl.

"Your Purity? You asked for me?"

"Open this chest," said the Emperor. "Open it even if you have to break it into pieces."

The strongman had brought his hammer, his chains, and his cast iron balls.

"I love breaking things, Your Glory," he said with a smile.

"Then break," said the Emperor.

The strongman lifted his heavy hammer . . .

Much later, when the cast iron balls had split and the chains and hammer had broken, the strongman burst into tears and wept. The chest was still intact.

"I don't understand, Your Excellency. It's the first time . . ."

The Emperor sighed.

"Have yourself whipped ten times. And tell the magician to make her way here."

"Your Elegance wants me to open this chest?" asked the magician.

"Yes. And fast."

"Consider it done."

"I've already heard that. Show me what you can do."

The magician leaned over the chest, throwing back her long red hair.

"*Paaalliaafichh! Ooffshtraach!* Chest, open up!"

Nothing happened. A touch of nervousness passed over the magician's face as the Emperor furrowed his brow.

"*Saalloooftee! Saalloooftaa!* Lock, open up!"

Still nothing. The magician was known for a thousand miles around, but the chest did not budge. The Emperor set a weary hand on her shoulder.

"Well. Ten lashes for you. Make sure they don't hold back, please. Oh, and call for the alchemist."

The alchemist's beard was so long that he often stepped on it. He spluttered as he entered the throne room.

"I demand that someone opens this chest for me," the Emperor groaned.

The alchemist rubbed his hands.

"Your Omnipotence, I have just the acids to work wonders on this!"

"Good. Then hurry up."

When the sun set, they lit torches to illuminate the throne room. The ground was full of holes from the acids the alchemist had used. Some of his concoctions were so corrosive that they burned through the floors of the castle until they reached the caves below. But the chest still looked brand new. And it remained closed.

"Have yourself lashed twenty times," said the Emperor.

"But the others only had to suffer ten!" the alchemist protested.

"Yes, but I'm angry. Twenty lashes will serve to relax me. Oh, and fetch me the . . ."

The Emperor didn't finish his sentence because, truth be told, he didn't know who else to ask to open the enchanted chest.

For weeks, the Emperor didn't sleep and barely ate. He thought only of the chest. What incredible wonders could it contain?

He sent word across the whole of his empire, promising a great reward to whoever could open the enchanted chest. But everyone knew what had happened, and nobody was in a rush to get whipped.

But then, one day, a young kitchen hand from the castle's kitchens appeared before the Emperor.

"Your Superiority, I'm sorry to disturb you, but I heard from the uncle of the friend of the brother of the dressmaker of the aunt of—"

"Enough! What? What is it, boy?"

"I learned that the wild lynx is capable of seeing through all things."

"So?"

"All things . . . even the walls of a chest, I imagine . . ."

In a flash, the Emperor leapt out of his throne.

"We must capture that lynx! We'll send a thousand hunters!"

The lynx was not easy to catch. She was a wild and cunning beast. But she was still captured. Once she was put in her cage, she listened to the conversations of the hunters as they brought her to the castle.

When she was presented to the Emperor, she already knew what was expected of her.

"Is it true," the Emperor asked, "that you can see through all things?"

"Yes, my boy," replied the lynx, who was not familiar with the policies of the court.

But the Emperor was too distracted by his obsession with the chest to take offense.

"For example," continued the lynx, "in the next room, behind that wall there, I see a woman sewing and a man polishing leather boots to make them shine."

With his voice trembling, the Emperor motioned to the chest.

"And what do you see in there, lynx? Nobody can open it."

It only took a moment for the animal and her magic eyes to discover what the chest held. Its metal walls were certainly thick, but inside it was entirely empty.

The lynx opened her mouth to tell the Emperor, but she remembered that sometimes the truth can be a dreadful thing, especially for whoever proclaims it.

"Well, I see—"

"Yes? Yes?"

"I see precious stones as large as apples. And necklaces made of pearls. And works wrought in gold. There's also an emerald the size of a melon. And a tiara inlaid with a thousand diamonds."

The Emperor raised his arms to the sky.

"I knew it! I was sure of it! An emerald the size of a melon, you said?"

"Maybe a little larger," the lynx murmured.

The liar was treated to a great feast of quail and pheasant, prepared by the very kitchen hand who had earned a promotion to head chef. The Emperor also declared that, in all his domain, lynx were never to be hunted again.

As for the chest, it rested in the castle's treasure room, under the constant watch of ten armed guards and a pack of fierce dogs. The Emperor would sometimes visit it; he would caress it and whisper sweet nothings to it.

Doesn't what we think we have matter just as much to us as what we really have?